Travel to Maurice's World!

Let your passport to adventure take you to Maurice's imaginary world online, beginning with Maurice's Secret Sycamore Tree app.

Additional apps take you inside each book in the *Maurice's Valises* series. Spend time in the playroom. Make friends and learn things from all over the world. Play fun games, earn mouse coins and moral badges, and collect your treasures in your own online valise. Use the special code below to begin. And even more activities are to come soon!

YOUR SPECIAL CODE
IS **BEE-KIND**

The Books Before...

In the Beginning
In the first book, Maurice, an orphan mouse, travels to New Zealand, where he is visited by the Muse of Mice and is given a great responsibility. Maurice learns the value of always telling the truth.

The Micetro of Moscow
In the second book, Maurice travels to Russia, where he befriends a musical (yet unpopular) mouse, Henry, who helps Tchaikovsky finish *Swan Lake*. Maurice learns that everyone is special in his or her own way.

Casablanca
In the third book, Maurice's adventures take him to Morocco, where a selfless act helps a bespectacled camel, Cecil, and Maurice learns the true meaning of friendship.

Medicine Mouse

In the fourth book, Maurice journeys to America. Traveling west, he befriends a kindly prairie dog, Pip, and meets a Medicine Mouse who shares his life's wisdom with Maurice.

Kookoo Mountain

In the fifth book, Maurice journeys to a hidden Alpine valley, where he meets Oswyn, a wise old owl, and learns a life lesson of questioning from this experience.

A Christmas Tail

In the sixth book, Maurice travels to Bavaria, where he encounters a circus elephant and an anteater, and he experiences the joy of giving to others.

The Books Before...

The Muuha of Bang Bua
In Maurice's seventh story, he survives an ocean voyage and a monsoon, and he reaches his journey's end on a sandbar in the middle of a river in Thailand. Maurice encounters the revered teacher Muuha and learns another important lesson of life.

The Beans of Budapest
In Maurice's eighth adventure, he finds himself becoming part of a gypsy family, where he learns the value and joy of teaching others.

Museum Mouse
The ninth book in the series, Maurice finds himself exploring the Egyptian Museum in Cairo, where he meets his Muse and learns about her darker side, the Muddler, and the real treasure of the Moral Scroll.

Kansas and the Crow
The tenth book in the series is a prairie odyssey in which the principles of compassion, charity, and planning for the future are revealed through the daily lives of animals living together by a secluded pond.

Chaturanga
The eleventh book in the series, Maurice's adventure transports him to a magical island fjord, and he comes to recognize that he is saved from danger through friendship and sacrifice.

What wisdom can you find that is greater than kindness?

—*Jean-Jacques Rousseau*

Forewords

"Teaching a child not to step on a caterpillar is as valuable to the child as it is to the caterpillar."

—Bradley Millar

Welcome to the amazing and magical world of Maurice, a place where caring and gratitude rule, and the real magic is the inspiring power of kindness. Jerry Friedman has created a world our children deserve—a world of possibilities, adventure, and compassion.

For children, stories are a way to inspire and generate imagination. As Maurice shares his journeys with family and friends, we are there with him: climbing mountains, saving the world, caring for our friends.

The value of these stories is the value of sharing—feeling what it means to be a true friend, doing what you know is the right thing, and treating others the way they would like to be treated.

Our children are growing up in a world different from the one in which we were raised. With increased ways of communicating have come challenges about what and how things are being said.

As we read the *Maurice* stories to our children, we reinforce the importance of being true to yourself and yet still finding ways to share your beliefs thoughtfully.

If something is worth being said, then isn't it worth being said so people can hear and understand?

Thank you for choosing this book to share with your child. We hope you both will share your stories with us.

—*Alice Cahn*
CahnWorks: Social Responsibility in Media

Forewords

One of the most important lessons we can teach our children is to be kind. While empathy and compassion may be present in children at a young age, these qualities require ongoing guidance and instruction in order to fully develop. Fortunately, there are many effective ways to teach kindness—including modeling kindness in our own interactions with adults and children, setting high and consistent standards for the caring behaviors of our children, and discussing fictional and real-life stories and examples of kindness.

At Making Caring Common, we believe that one of the most important things parents can do to cultivate kindness and empathy is to discuss and practice caring behaviors with their children. This includes helping kids extend whom they care about (their "Circle of Concern") beyond those they know well and like, to include those that are different from them in background and beliefs and for whom showing compassion and kindness may be a much more difficult task.

While it may sound obvious, it's important to tell children that "being kind to everyone" is important and highly valued, and to ask about and recognize acts of kindness and injustice in the home, community, and world. Without these practices and expectations, kindness can get "lost" in the shuffle of the day to day and drowned out by messages about the importance of high achievement or personal happiness.

J.S. Friedman's colorful new tale, *The Book of Beeing*, provides parents and young people with a gateway to these challenging and important conversations. Embedded in Maurice's animated adventure is the message that kindness to everyone matters. In *The Book of Beeing*, kindness is not only key to finding the treasure and pursuing one's goal, but ultimately is the most important goal and a treasure in and of itself.

—Dr. Richard Weissbourd/Making Caring Common
http://mcc.gse.harvard.edu

www.mauricesvalises.com

ISBN: 978-94-91613-22-7-50799

MOUSE PRINTS PRESS

Prinsengracht 1053-S Boot
1017 JE Amsterdam Netherlands

Maurice's Valises

Moral Tails in an Immoral World

Forewords by Alice Cahn
& Dr. Richard Weissbourd

The Book of Beeing

By J. S. Friedman
Illustrations by Chris Beatrice

A swarm of 98 little grandmice and their forest friends pounded on the snowy door.

From inside they could hear "I'm coming, be patient" as the door flew open and there stood Maurice, the teller of tales, silhouetted by the light of his den's fireplace. The little ones zoomed by Maurice and settled into a pile of mufflers and boots, at the foot of his old, worn chair.

As always, his storytelling chair sat in the center of Maurice's den, in the base of an old sycamore tree, deep in the woods.

"Is Grandwald here, number 79?" asked Maurice.

"Buzzz" came a laugh from Grandwald, the sweetest, giantest mouse of the forest.

"Is Tiny here?" asked Maurice again.

"Buzzz, buzzz," said Tiny with a titter as she climbed aboard Grandwald's lap.

"And have my nieces paid me a visit?" asked Maurice.

"We're here," hummed the little voices of Mya, Molly, and Marigold.

"Well then, call me Maurice," said Grandpa to the group. "I suppose there's no point in my leaning on my walking stick when I could be sitting."

And so, that was that—he sat.

Tonight, Maurice was his usual jolly self, but there was something different.

He moved a little slower than usual. He leaned on his walking stick with a little more weight and sank into his seat with a sizeable sigh.

"So, my little kerchiefed girls, why don't you pick a story tonight?"

"Can you tell us the one about to bees or not to bees and the lost shell?"

"You mean the bees of Machu Picchu?" said Maurice.

"Why, of course."

"Buzzz, buzzz, buzzz" buzzed the whole room with giggles of agreement.

Maurice turned to the tall stack of luggage behind him, and with a mighty tug he pulled at a rather large valise near the bottom of the pile.

As always, they came tumbling down, and Maurice disappeared under the suitcases. He popped up with a smile and the handle of the valise.

Maurice stood surrounded by his life's trusty travel companions. He opened the one stickered "Machu Picchu," and out came a brightly colored poncho, a chullo, a fuzzy blanket, AND 12 tiny Golden Scrolls. 🐾

On went the clothes, across his lap went the blanket, and across his face went a big smile as he sat in his storytelling chair.

PAW NOTE

 A poncho is a blanket-like outer garment, used to keep warm.

PAW NOTE

 A chullo is an Andean-style woven hat with earflaps, used to keep the head warm.

PAW NOTE

 Golden Scrolls were the original Scrolls with wise sayings written on them. They foretold the the traveling tales of a Chosen One.

"So," began Maurice," once upon a time, I made my home in a wonderful wooden box stuffed with sweet-smelling shavings, which sat in the basement of a school. Very comfortable and snuggly warm.

"One morning, I was awakened by arguing adults, as my box lid was removed and long metal cylinders *(binoculars)* were placed on top of me. I was squished.

"Then a layer of papers and maps was also placed on top.

Then the lid was replaced, and the box was clasped under the arguing arm of Quentin Quarrel, an archeologist. 🐾

"I heard him hiss his orders to a group of international expeditionists *(and plunderers)*—then off the box and I went. Endless bumpety bump days and rockety rock nights stretched into a longety long time."

PAW NOTE

An archaeologist is a person who studies ancient and recent human history through material remains.

"One day, all the bumpeties came to an end. I felt like I was hoisted into the air. Then I heard a new language spoken.

I heard Spanish shouts and the *clackety clack* of hooves on stones, and many *mew* sounds could be heard from a herd."

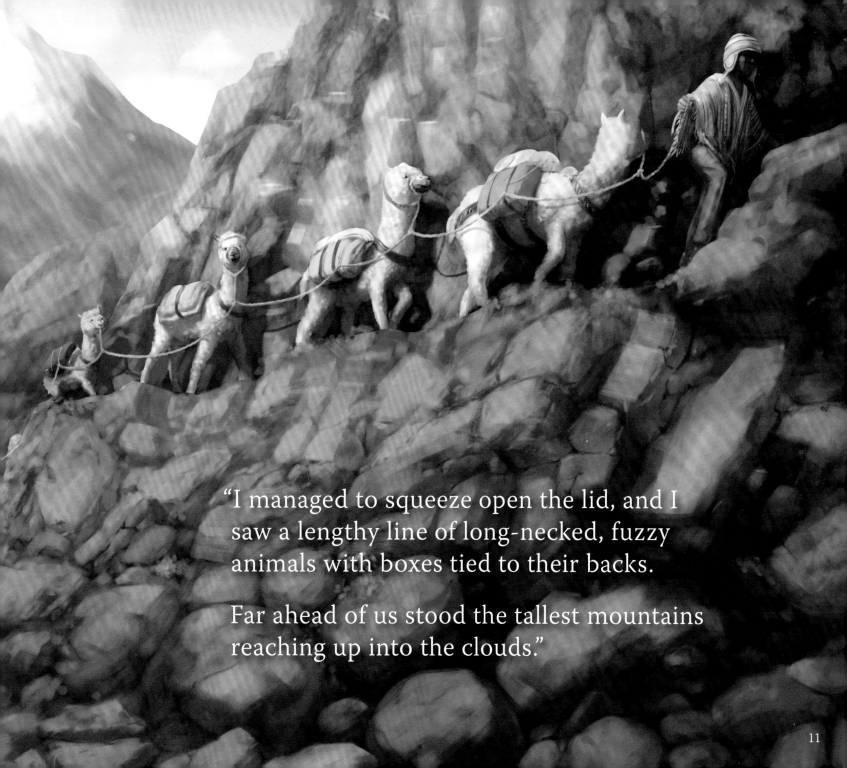

"I managed to squeeze open the lid, and I saw a lengthy line of long-necked, fuzzy animals with boxes tied to their backs.

Far ahead of us stood the tallest mountains reaching up into the clouds."

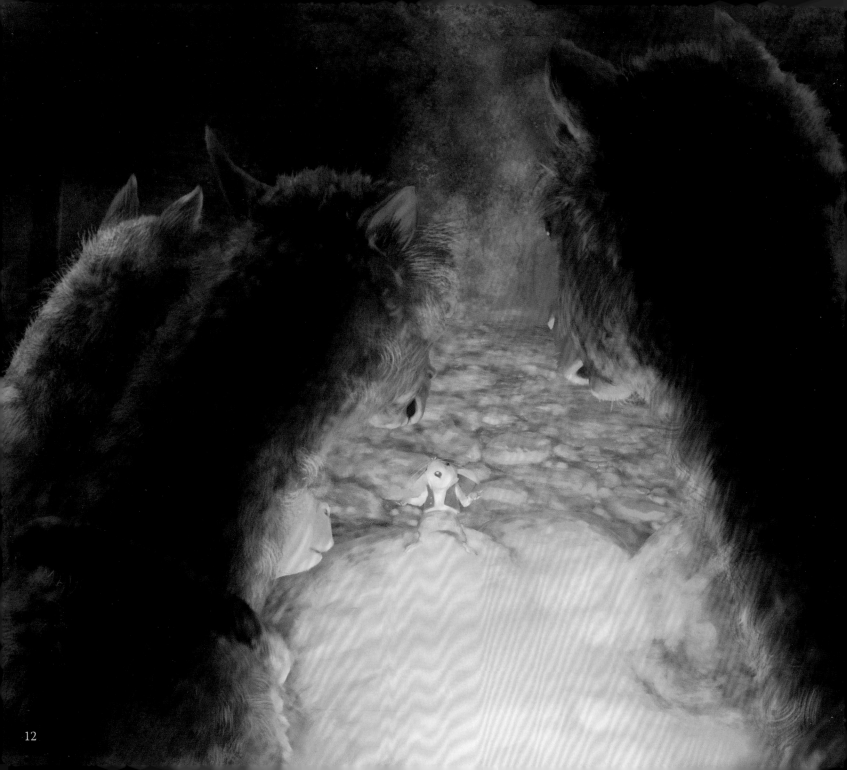

"That night, I snuck out to get some food and water. I found I was at a campfire encircled with closed-eyed llamas chewing and mewing.

"I spoke to the first one who opened his (or her) eyes.

"'Hi, I'm Maurice.'

"'Hello, I'm Al, and so is he, and she and she and he and all the rest,' said Al.

"'What?' I said. 'You're all named Al?'

"'Yup, that's our name. Al is our first; Paka is our last.

"'What's *your* last name?' mewed Al.

"'I'm not sure I have one,' I said. Then I replied, 'Maybe Ofthevalise.'"

"'And where did you come from, Ofthevalise?' asked Al.

"'From a coconut shell,' I said. When Al heard *shell*, he asked, 'Are you going to look for "The Shell" too?'

"What shell?" I asked.

"'Why, the lost legend See Shell that the ancients hid up in their mountain city of Machu Picchu.

"'That's where we're going with this bickering bunch of men who can't ever agree on anything and who are making us carry all of this heavy scientific equipment,' Al said.

"And at daybreak, we were on our way again."

"Bumping and swaying up narrow paths cut into the mountains, I pushed the lid off my box and peeked a few times to see where we were going.

"Dizzying depths below and perpendicular paths above. I could hear the rush-gush of water falling to the valley floor.

"I could hear the arguing of the humans again, each saying who was going to find the treasure shell first.

"All of the Als muttered and sputtered, noses to tails, as they made their trek up the well-worn, stony trail in a winding line. They had trudged this trail so many times, it was like a memory march."

"The second night of the trek I again spent talking to all of the Als.

I learned that the ancients had long since disappeared from the mountain city after wrangling times of war, and that the city had once been the center of a great civilization that had vanished along with the See."

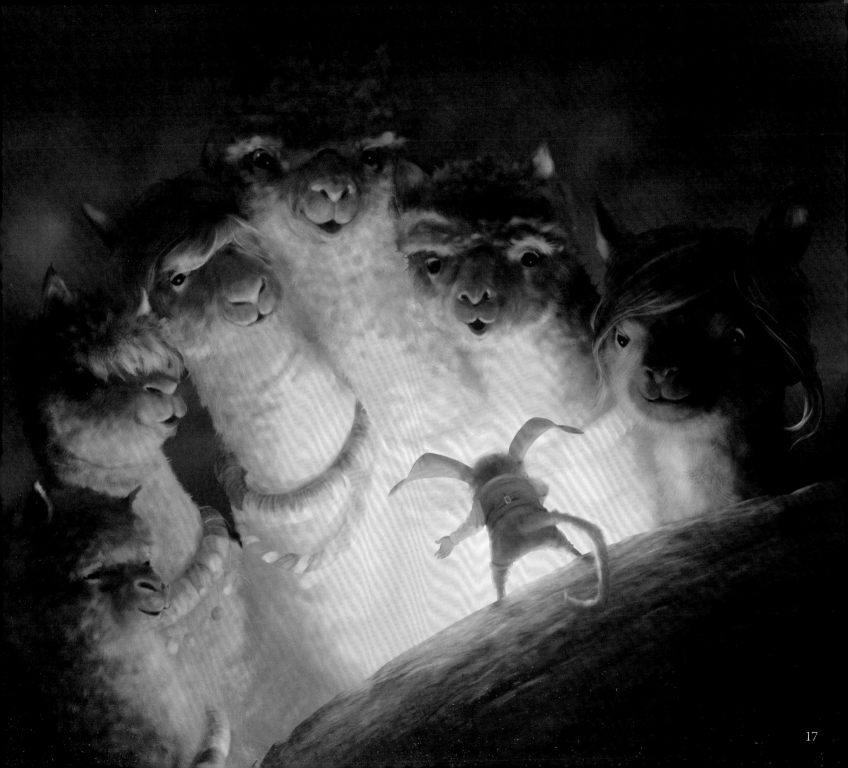

"According to legend, the king had left a golden See Shell hidden inside another giant shell. The golden shell was blown to assemble the people to see what they could see.

This shell also held all their visions of life and was hidden where it would always bee protected.

"I couldn't understand where the water had gone, if there had been a sea way up here. How could you lose it? How could a sea dry up? Or down?

"I kept thinking and thinking until I couldn't think any more, and then I heard the voice of my Muse, soft like the wind, whisper to me."

"'Maurice, Maurice, you and I are almost at your journey's end—bee aware, bee wise, and you will gain conchousness.'

"As always, no one heard the Muse but me.

"The Als stared at me. They chewed and mewed. They had to go to sleep. The next day's climb would be hard until we reached the city of Machu Picchu, and then they could graze as the men squabbled and searched.

"At noon, we had almost reached the summit when my box became unstrapped and tumbled off the back of my Al."

"The box and I crashed to the ground.

"The lid popped open. I watched as the binoculars bounced and the maps fluttered away until they disappeared over the edge of the path.

"The scientists scrambled and ran, but they were too late."

"The quarreling began. Professor Quentin hissed his orders.

"I climbed up an Al's tail and hid.

"After a while, the grumbling march continued up the hill.

"When we reached the path's end, the mountain city lay perched on the edge of a cliff, the equipment was piled up in the stone square, and the scientists started their mapless search.

"It was only when I saw the scientists running from a little dark, moving cloud that I realized they were running away from a swarm of bees.

"The bees must have been protecting their hive."

"As I got closer to the edge of the town's cliff, I saw an old, twisted tree growing from the top of a pinnacle of rock about 50 feet away. Tangled vines grew like a twisty bridge across the empty space above the valley."

"Into this tree the swarm disappeared.

"Something shiny was wedged in the tree,
covered with flowers *(and bees)."*

25

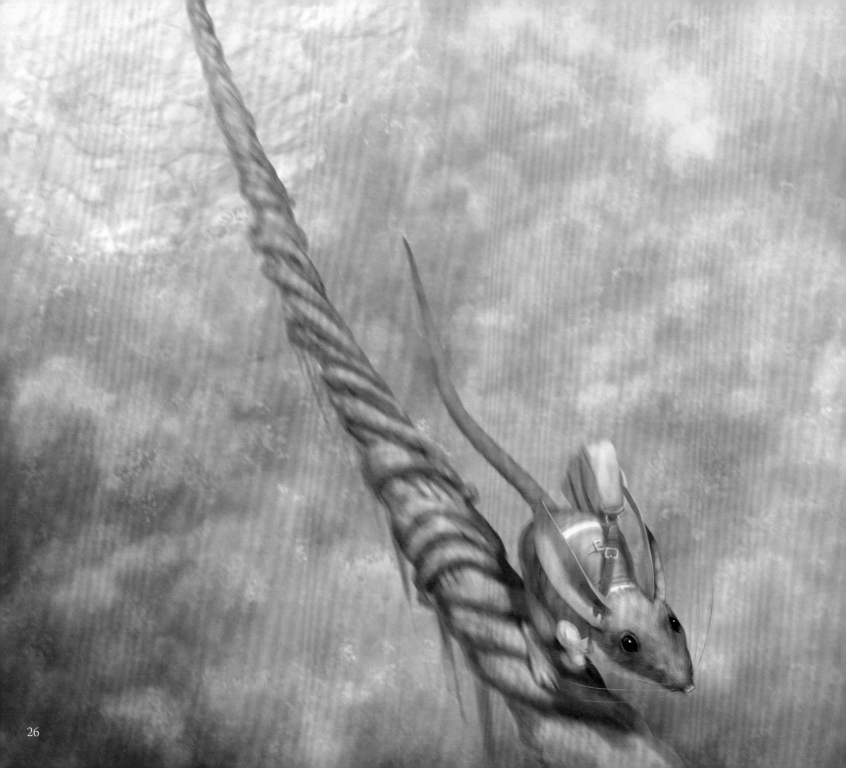

"Following the Muse's wise words to bee aware, I scampered over the woven vine bridge *(and tried not to look down to the valley floor way below)* to see what I could see, as the hum grew louder and louder.

"The *buzzz buzzz buzzz* was all I could hear. And then it stopped."

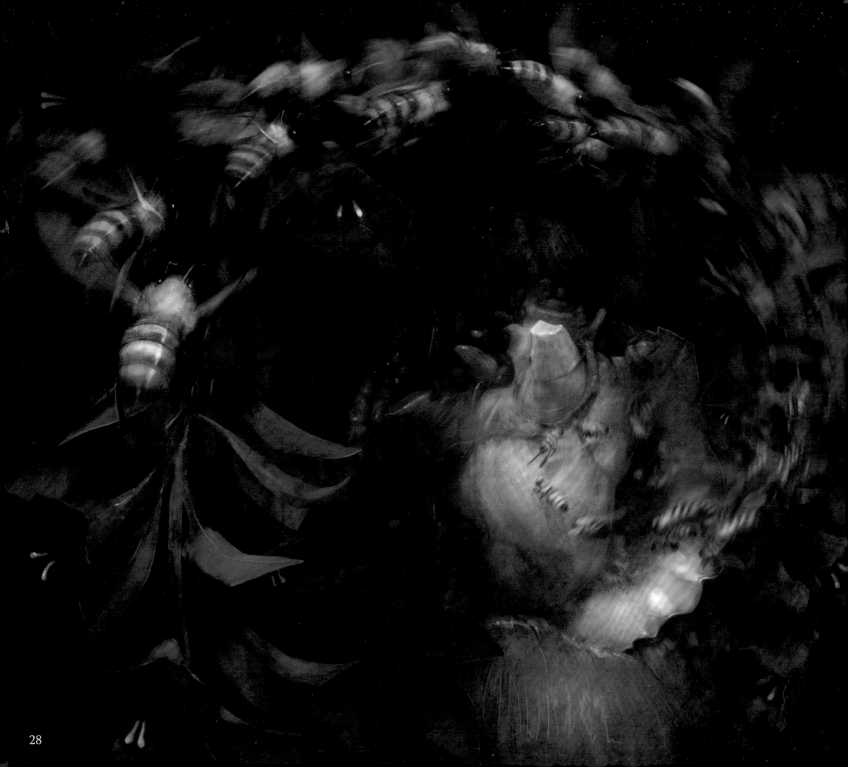

"The bees disappeared through the flowered vines covering an entrance to the tree's hollow—but it wasn't a hollow. It was the opening of a prehistoric giant conch shell, imbedded in this ancient tree.

"As I crept through the flowers, the hum began again.

"On the sidewall of the shell were scratched symbols and pictures.

"There in the deep back of the chamber was a skep, and next to it a neat pile of the tiniest, tied Golden Scrolls and a beautiful, gleaming golden conch shell."

PAW NOTE
A skep is a beehive from ancient times.

"The Queen of the bees, Beeatrice, sat surrounded by soldier bees whose wings fanned her and made the humming sound."

Maurice paused his memories for a moment. He looked around the room at the faces of his grandmice and his nieces and their forest friends.

They were frozen with anticipation as Maurice tried to remember all the facts he had learned.

"Did you know, little ones," began Maurice again, "that bees have been around since the dinosaurs?

"Or that each and every bee's role is important to the survival of the colony?

"And did you know that bees are the most efficient builders in the world?

"Or that honeybees communicate distance and the direction of pollen by dancing?"

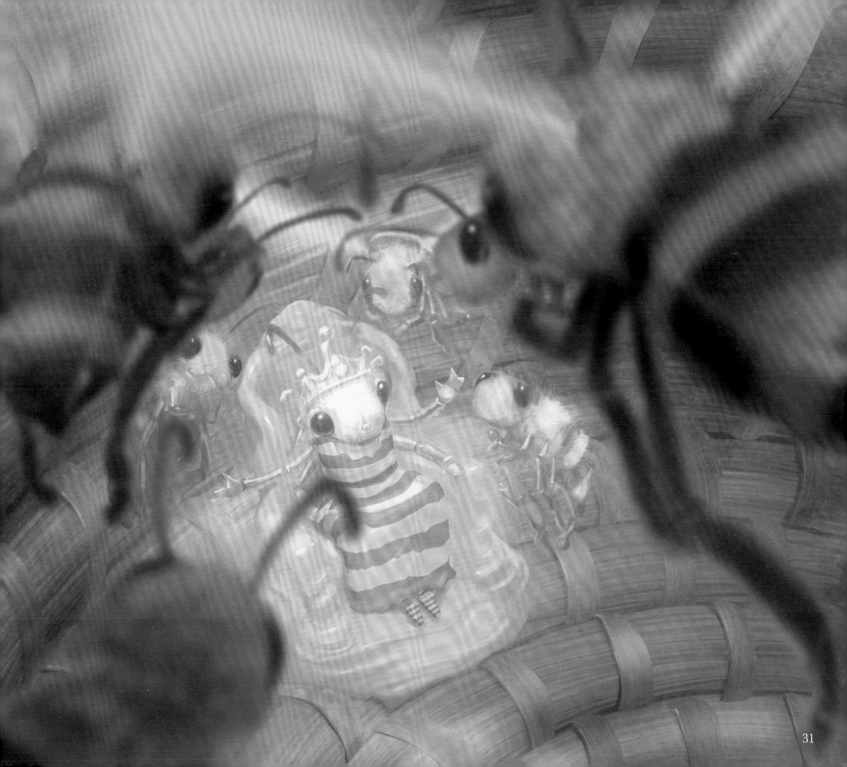

No one stirred. No one buzzed. Everyone silently stared at Maurice.

Maurice continued. . . .

"The Queen bee, Beeatrice, looked out at me and, just like the Muse, spoke without speaking. I heard what she said in my head.

"'My, my, it has taken a long, long time for you to come. . . .' said Queen Beeatrice.

"'We have been protecting these Scrolls for many centuries.

"'We have lived here, generation after generation, protecting these vision Scrolls and the golden conch.

The ancients called this the See Shell.'"

"'Ever since the ancient wise ones left for good, we have been entrusted with these wisdom Scrolls, for others to live by. . . . The ancients predicted you would come someday.

"'You see, Maurice of the Valise, wisdom—like pollination—must be spread around for the good of all. The ancient ones learned from us, from our compassionate ways, and put this knowledge down in their Moral Scrolls for all to benefit.

"'And we have kept these golden rolls—these Scrolls—hidden, so that they couldn't be taken or destroyed because they belong to all, not to a few.

And now, they are for *you* to protect and cherish.'"

"'The ancient ones loved us, we bees, not because of our honey-making powers, but because of the power of our harmony, our wisdom, our honesty, our sacrifice.

"'They even made hats that looked like hives to sit on their heads. See, on the walls—they scratched and drew pictures of their teachers wearing the hats,' Beeatrice said.

"When I looked at the wall pictures—which were like picture books, with stories of the ancient ones in beehive hats and with Golden Scrolls—the stories came alive."

"Scenes of farming, animals that lived long ago, and wars that ended in tears were painted in bright colors.

"The ancient ones even painted their own passing. They knew that as a people of peace, they would not endure.

"But they had dreams—they wrote of their hopes for kindness, for kind men, which became the human word 'mankind.'

"The Muse whispered to me again: 'Maurice, carry the Scrolls to safety, and seek and settle deep in a distant forest.'"

"With that I gathered up all the Golden
Scrolls into my valise, leaving the golden
shell behind.

"I scurried out of the giant conch shell, crossed
the vine bridge, and chewed through the
woven stems.

"The severed bridge fell away. The golden
conch was protected."

"I climbed aboard one the Als' backs, and with the glowing swarm of soldier bees assembled around me, we set off down the mountain in search of this forest.

"As I looked back, I could see the archaeologists beeing chased back and forth.

"Even Quentin Quarrel, now surrounded with a swirling black cloud of bees, dared not follow as the huge humming protected me, my valise, and the Golden Scrolls all the way down to the bottom of the mountain and to the journey's end—and to our special, secret sycamore tree."

Silence.

Not a titter, a whisper, nor a *buzzz* could be heard from the den. Grandwald hugged Tiny tightly. Then Mya, Molly, and Marigold spoke up.

"Is that the end?"

"What does the Moral Scroll say?"

Maurice unrolled his last Moral Scroll. His smile touched each and every one in the room.

He read:

To bee or not to bee
is not the question, for
To bee is to bee kind, and the
greatest form of wisdom
is kindness.

Maurice already had his head tilted in his chair, eyes closed, ready for a special snooze.

He popped open one eye, one last time, just to look around, then sank into the deepest, softest, slumbered snore, *buzzz/hum, buzzz/hum ... buzzz ... hummmmmmm.*

The three nieces leaned over Maurice, and, one by one, each touched noses with him.

A bolt of Maurice's knowledge passed to each one, like the wise Medicine Mouse before them. As Maurice's snores snored on, the Muse of Mice appeared to Maurice once again. Softly she spoke, with a smile.

She whispered sweet words of wisdom:

"So now you know, Maurice, I am you and you are me, and we are so, together. Let us bee.

"We shall go on and on, so sleep.

"We are the eternal keepers of the Scrolls."

Maurice, eyes shut, could hear the faraway lapping of ocean's waves on a distant shore. He could see himself appearing in his mind, a faint image of a little mouse rocking in the ocean in his coconut shell.

"Let's rest now," said the voice of the Muse.

"We will soon return, you and I; for us there's always more to come."

The end. But really, there is no end . . . only

In the Beginning. . . .

Contributor Biographies

Alice Cahn is a media, education, and social responsibility executive. Recent experience includes Turner Broadcasting's Cartoon Network, creating content and projects that increased audiences, reversed negative youth and adult attitudes about youth brands, and built effective partnerships with business, government, education, and advocacy and community-based organizations. A frequent speaker at conferences on digital media and communicating to parents and youth, she serves on the advisory boards of several foundations and associations.

Dr. Richard Weissbourd is currently a lecturer in education at the Harvard Kennedy School of Education and at the Kennedy School of Government. He is also Faculty Director of the Human Development and Psychology master's program. His work focuses on vulnerability and resilience in childhood, the achievement gap, moral development, and effective schools and services for children.

map of
Maurice's
Travels

North America

South America

Europe

Africa

Asia

Australia

Questions to Chew On

During this story, there are many examples of "alliteration." Alliteration is when two or more words in a row have the same beginning sound, like "seven swimming swans." Go back into the story and find as many of these examples as you can.

Can you find alliteration in some other stories or poems that you have read? What makes alliteration so interesting? Think of some of your own. Write a poem or story with your own examples.

Maurice's nieces' names all begin with the letter M. Can you think of any names that begin with the first letter of your name? You can make up some new ones too!

Why was Maurice moving a little slower and leaning on his walking stick? Why do you sometimes move a bit slower than usual?

During this story, Maurice was squished under a pair of binoculars. What are those, and when would you use them?

How funny that all of the llamas were named Al!! What problems might arise if all of your friends had the same name? How could you solve those problems?

Bees are very good at protecting their hives. How do other animals protect their homes and habitats? How do humans do that?

The Queen of the bees was named Beeatrice . . . an alliterative name. Remember alliteration? What could you name other animal Queens that would follow that same rule? My example is Lily Lion!

Bees are such interesting insects—each has his own job to do, and they are all experts! Plus they have been around since the dinosaurs! What do you think they looked like back then? Draw a picture.

Why was it so important for Maurice to protect the Scrolls?

"Wisdom—like pollination—must be spread around for the good of all," said a wise one. What other characteristics should be spread around like pollen? Why?

Do you know of other people who painted on the walls of their homes? What did the paintings mean?

Part of the Moral Scroll for this story says "the greatest form of wisdom is kindness." Do you agree? Why?

The Moral Scroll says "To bee or not to bee is not the question, for to bee is to bee kind, and the greatest form of wisdom is kindness."

What is so important about wisdom? What does it mean to you? How do you feel when you are kind?

Postscript

The Book of Beeing is the last book in my *Maurice's Valises* series, and, like the previous books in the collection, it is my attempt to reach back to my childhood and pull feelings, thoughts, and questions forward into the present to inspire children.

Blended with a deeper understanding of kindness from the legacy of a lifetime is this collaborative adventure which I have been fortunate to share with Chris Beatrice, the artist, who painted my words.

My hope is that some enquiring child out there reads or hears these stories, journeys through his or her imagination, and has the chance to curiously dream as I have dreamt.

—*JSF*

Acknowledgments

As I have done before in my previous 11 books, I wish to thank my team of helpers, without whom I could not have published this book and completed this series.

My warmest thanks, as always to Elías R. Ragnarsson in Reykjavik, my time zone traveler and teammate for his diligence and tolerance in working strange hours on Skype to complete this project. Additionally, thank you for your forbearance in the face of constantly changing layouts and copy.

Many thanks to Stephanie Arnold for her early editorial contributions and to Renee Rooks Cooley for her meticulous attention to detail and copyediting expertise. To Paula Prentiss for her educational questions and to Marion Pothoff in Amsterdam for her expert eye in pre-press preparations.

To my wife, Cheryl, thank you for your patience in sharing our lives on Maurice's monumental marathon.

And what more can I say but take a bow, Chris Beatrice. My many thanks to you, my colleague of imagination who translated my musings, visualized my words, and transformed my dreams into art.